What about Bear?

Suzanne Bloom

ALANNA BOOKS

Let's play.

Sure. Jump right in.

I want to play a
different game.

What about Bear?

Bear is
too big.

I want to play
a new game.

What about Bear?

Bear is too
grumpy.

I want to play
another new
game.

What about Bear?

Bear is too
far away.

But Bear
is my friend.
Wait, Bear!
Come back!

What about me?

Bear is my big, old
sometimes grumpy
friend.
You can be our
new friend.

So, do you want
to play with us?

Yes. I do.

OK.
Jump right in!